Farmyard Tales

Tractor in Trouble

Heather Amery

Adapted by Rob Lloyd Jones

Illustrated by Stephen Cartwright

Reading consultant: Alison Kelly

Find the duck on every double page.

This story is about Apple Tree Farm,

Sam,

Poppy,

Farmer
Dray's
farm

Apple Tree
Station

Apple Tree
Village

Church

School

Manor

Ted,

Farmer
Dray,

Dolly

and a
tractor.

It was a windy day on
Apple Tree Farm.

Sam and Poppy were
playing in the barn.

A tractor rumbled past.

Ted was going to mend
the sheep shed.

Ted climbed onto
the roof.

The wind blew stronger
and stronger...

At the barn, Sam and
Poppy heard a CRASH!

A tree had fallen over and landed on Ted's tractor.

"My poor tractor," sighed Ted. It was trapped under the tree.

Farmer Dray knew
what to do.

He brought his chain
saw and his horse, Dolly.

First, he cut up the tree.

13

Then Dolly dragged the branches away.

One of the branches
was very heavy.

Dolly heaved
and heaved...

At last, she pulled the branch away.

Finally Ted could climb back into his tractor.

Thank you Farmer Dray.

Now the tractor needs
some new paint.

You missed
a patch.

It needs a polish too.

But maybe when it's
not so windy...

Puzzles

Puzzle 1

Put the five pictures in order.

A.

B.

C.

D.

E.

Puzzle 2

Pick the best word to describe Poppy and Sam in each picture.

A.

sleeping   playing   fighting

B.

flying   sitting   running

Puzzle 3

Can you spot five differences between these two pictures?

Puzzle 4

Choose the right sentence for each picture.

A.

It was a windy day.
It was a rainy day.

B.

A racing car sped past.
A tractor rumbled past.

C.

First he had a cup of tea.
First he cut up the tree.

D.

Sam and Poppy heard a crash.
Sam and Poppy heard a splash.

Answers to puzzles
Puzzle 1

1E.

2B.

3A.

4C.

5D.

Puzzle 2

A.

playing

B.

running

Puzzle 3

Puzzle 4

A. It was a
   windy day.

B. A tractor
   rumbled past.

C. First he cut
   up the tree.

D. Sam and
   Poppy heard
   a crash.

Designed by Laura Nelson
Series editor: Lesley Sims
Series designer: Russell Punter
Digital manipulation by Nick Wakeford

This edition first published in 2016 by Usborne Publishing Ltd.,
Usborne House, 83-85 Saffron Hill, London EC1N 8RT, England.
www.usborne.com Copyright © 2016, 1990 Usborne Publishing Ltd.

USBORNE FIRST READING
Level Two

USBORNE FIRST READING

Farmyard Tales

Pig Gets Stuck

Illustrated by Stephen Cartwright

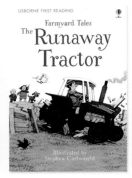

USBORNE FIRST READING

Farmyard Tales

The Runaway Tractor

Illustrated by Stephen Cartwright

USBORNE FIRST READING

Farmyard Tales

The Naughty Sheep

Illustrated by Stephen Cartwright

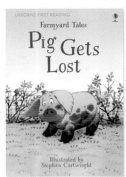

USBORNE FIRST READING

Farmyard Tales

Pig Gets Lost

Illustrated by Stephen Cartwright

USBORNE FIRST READING

Farmyard Tales

Scarecrow's Secret

Illustrated by Stephen Cartwright

USBORNE FIRST READING

One, Two, Buckle My Shoe

Retold by Russell Punter
Illustrated by David Semple

USBORNE FIRST READING

There Was A Crooked Man

Retold by Russell Punter
Illustrated by David Semple

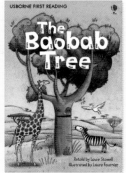

USBORNE FIRST READING

The Baobab Tree

Retold by Louie Stowell
Illustrated by Laure Fournier

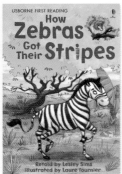

USBORNE FIRST READING

How Zebras Got Their Stripes

Retold by Lesley Sims
Illustrated by Laure Fournier